# JUNKET IS NICE

## by Dorothy Kunhardt

The New York Review Children's Collection
New York

THIS IS A NEW YORK REVIEW BOOK
PUBLISHED BY THE NEW YORK REVIEW OF BOOKS
435 Hudson Street, New York, NY 10014
www.nyrb.com

Published by permission of Penk, Inc.

Library of Congress Cataloging-in-Publication Data

Kunhardt, Dorothy, 1901–1979.
 Junket is nice / by Dorothy Kunhardt.
    p. cm. — (New York Review children's collection)
 Summary: All the world puzzles over what an old man with a red beard and red slip-
pers thinks about while eating an enormous bowl of a custard-like treat, but it is a little
boy on a tricycle who solves the riddle.
 ISBN 978-1-59017-628-3 (alk. paper)
[1. Desserts—Fiction. 2. Riddles—Fiction. 3. Humorous stories.]  I. Title.
 PZ7.K94904Ju 2013
 [E]—dc23
                                    2012035497

ISBN 978-1-59017-628-3

Cover design by Louise Fili Ltd.

Printed in the United States on acid-free paper.
0 9 8 7 6 5 4 3 2 1

Once there was an old old man with a red beard and red slippers. He was sitting at a table eating out of a big red bowl. He was eating junket out of the big red bowl. The old man ate and ate and ate. More junket and more junket and more junket and more junket until at last people began to be very much surprised at how much junket he was eating and they began to tell their friends about him because he seemed to be such a very hungry old man. So people and their friends began coming to look at the old man eating his junket.

First all the people who could run

very fast and their friends came.

Then all the people who could run

just a little fast and their friends came.

Then all the people who could only

walk and their friends came

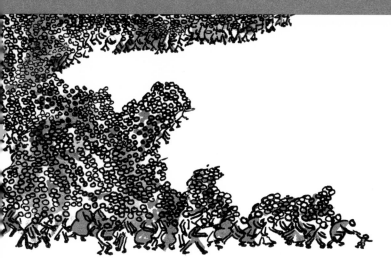

and last of all came a little boy
on a tricycle and the little boy on a
tricycle rode right up to where the

old man was eating and eating his

junket. And after that no more

people came because there were

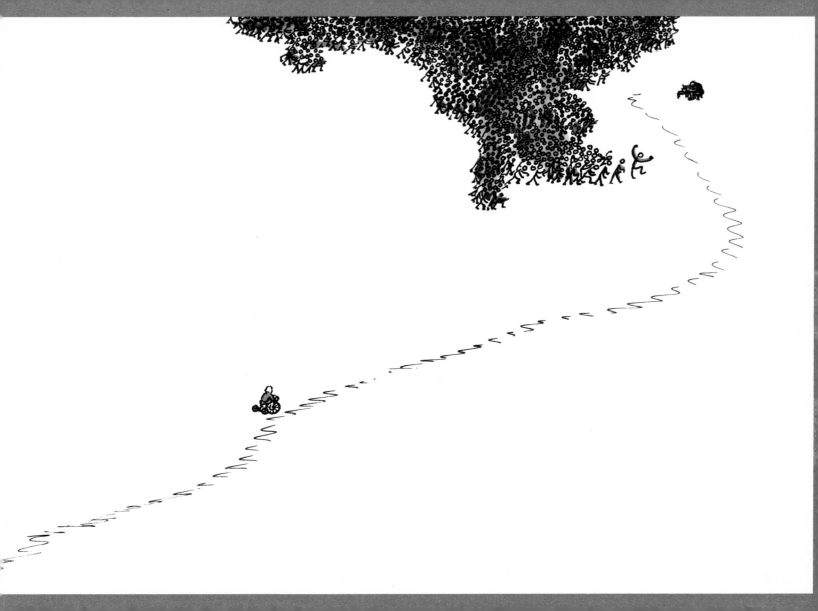

no more people. Every single person in the world was right there watching the old man eat his junket. And as soon as the old man saw that all the people in the world were there he stopped eating. his junket. But he was only stopping because he wanted to say something to all the people in the world and he said People why don't you try and guess what I am thinking about all the time I am eating my junket and if you guess right I will give you something nice. Then he made a

smiling Face and he said Now don't guess yet because first I am going to give you a little help. I am going to tell you three things that I am NOT thinking about ·········· and I really and truly am NOT.

I am NOT thinking about

a   walrus   with   an   apple   on   his   back.


And   I'm   NOT   thinking   about

a one year old lion blowing out the candle on his lovely birthday cake.

And I'm NOT thinking about

a cow with her head in a bag

. . . . . .

And those were the three things that
the old man was NOT thinking about
and as soon as the old man had
finished telling the three things he went on
eating his junket.　　Then all the people

in the world said Well if the old man is not thinking about a walrus with an apple on his back and if he is not thinking about a one year old lion blowing out the candle on his lovely birthday cake and if he is not thinking about a cow with her head in a bag . then that makes it VERY EASY

We will just guess EVERYTHING except a walrus with an apple on his back and except a one year old lion blowing out the candle on his lovely birthday cake and except a cow with her head in a bag. So all the people in the world began to guess and someone guessed a Kangaroo jumping over a glass of orange juice so as not to spill it.

WRONG! said the old man and he went on eating his junket.

And someone quessed

a daddy-long-legs    holding  up  his

foot    for    the    sun    to    warm    it .

# WRONG! said the old

man  and   he  went  on   eating   his  junket.

Then    someone  guessed

a pig seeing how many minutes
it takes for a cold bath.

WRONG! said the old man

and he went on eating his junket.

And then someone guessed

a camel practicing humming a song and the troublesome thing is having so much smoke from the fire when smoke is even worse than anything for humming.

WRONG! said the old man and he went on eating his junket.

And then someone guessed

a deer with Christmas tree things on his horns waiting around the corner to surprise Santa Claus.

WRONG! said the old man and he went on eating his junket.

And then someone guessed

a hippopotamus with all the lights turned out laughing at how hard it is to see the other people on the sofa.

WRONG! said the old man and he went on eating his junket.

And then someone guessed

a vulture looking all around the rocks for five lumps of sugar but I suppose he's forgotten about the one on the top of his head.

WRONG! said the old man and he went on eating his junket.

Then someone guessed

a sheep deciding to jump down now in case of night coming.

WRONG! said the old man and he went on eating his junket.

Then someone guessed

a tiger creeping past the door on tiptoe because the rule is no tigers clattering about at baby's nap time.

WRONG! said the old man and he went on eating his junket.

And then someone guessed

a pelican pretending he did'nt hear anybody call him.

WRONG! said the old man and he went on eating his junket.

And then someone quessed

a bear climbing a ladder because his toenails are too long for walking on the ground.

WRONG! said the old man and he went on eating his junket.

Then someone guessed

a rabbit wondering if there can be
a bunch of grapes tied to his tail.

WRONG! said the old man
and he went on eating his junket.

Now all the time that all the people in
the world were guessing and guessing the
little boy on a tricycle was thinking and
thinking and he was thinking that all

the people in the world were very silly people. He was thinking that they were very silly people to quess so many WRONG things and all of a sudden the little boy on a tricycle rode his tricycle right up to the old man who was eating and eating his junket and he said Old man, I know what you are thinking about all the time you are eating your junket. and the old man said Well what? and the little boy on a tricycle said Old man you are thinking about

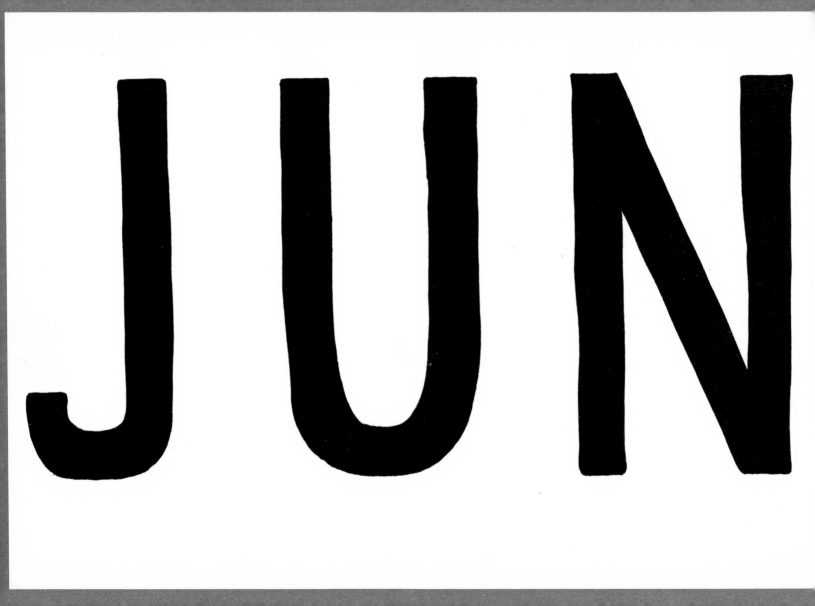

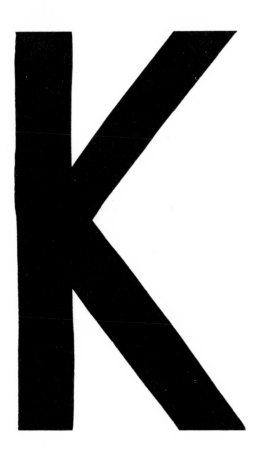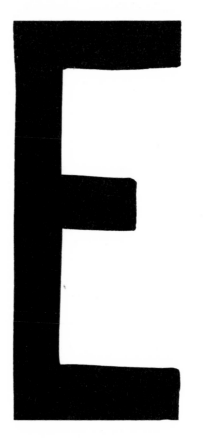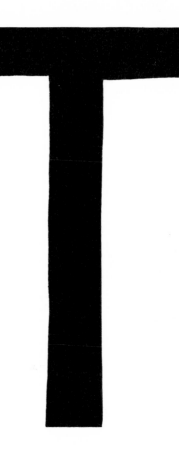

RIGHT! said the old man and qlup! he ate up the very last bite of junket that was in the big red bowl and when he saw that he had eaten up the very last bite of junket that was in the big red bowl he said Oh what a pity well no matter we can manage and he said Well Well little boy I said I would so I will give you SOMETHING NICE and he said Well Well Well little boy you look like a good

# LICKER

so just go ahead and lick little boy and lick and you can lick the bottom and you can lick the sides and you can lick round and round and round. So the little boy on a tricycle got off his tricycle and he was a good licker and he licked and licked and he licked the bottom and he licked the sides and he licked round and round and round and then he said Oh my but junket is nice! But all

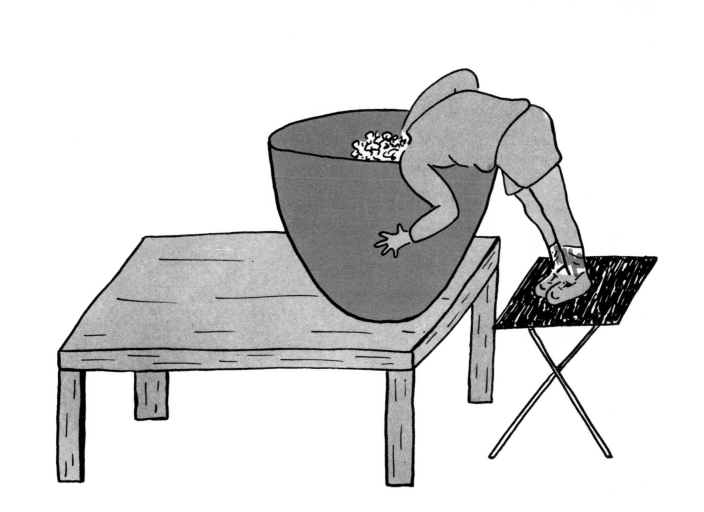

the people in the world were very angry and they stamped their feet and while they were stamping their feet they said Oh dear it isn't fair for a little boy to have all that nice licking why we were just guessing all those old guesses for fun why we knew it was junket all the time. But the old man said now people try to be a good sport because you can't fool me but I will say guessing is very hard to do and sometimes I think it is all LUCK anyway. But all the people in the world were still angry and they went on stamping their feet. Then the old man said Well goodbye little boy I must be getting home to my supper and as soon as the old man said Well goodbye little boy the little boy said Well goodbye old man and the old man said That looks like a good strong tricycle you have little boy and the little boy said Yes good and strong and the old man said It's too bad I'll be pretty late for my supper unless

I happen to get a ride home on somebody's tricycle. And the little boy on a tricycle said HOP ON old man so the old man hopped on and the little boy on a tricycle gave the old man with a red beard and red slippers a ride home to his SUPPER and all the time that they were riding home to the old man's supper the old man said Oh My Oh my Oh my Oh my Oh my but

JUNKET

IS

NICE !

**DOROTHY MESERVE KUNHARDT** (1901–1979) was an American author of books for small children and is best known for *Pat the Bunny* (1940), one of the all-time best-selling children's books in the United States. Her first book, *Junket Is Nice*, was a success when it appeared in 1933 and was followed by *Now Open the Box* (forthcoming from The New York Review Children's Collection), *Lucky Mrs. Ticklefeather*, *Brave Mr. Buckingham*, and *Tiny Animal Stories*. Kunhardt published nearly fifty books, including several nonfiction works for adults about Abraham Lincoln and the Civil War (her father amassed a legendary collection of Civil War–era photographs and memorabilia). Several years after her death, Philip B. Kunhardt Jr. remembered his mother's boundless curiosity and appreciation for the way young people observe the world, writing in *The New York Times* that "for Dorothy Kunhardt a children's book was nothing more or less than a way to talk to children."

## TITLES IN THE NEW YORK REVIEW CHILDREN'S COLLECTION

**ESTHER AVERILL**

*Captains of the City Streets*

*The Hotel Cat*

*Jenny and the Cat Club*

*Jenny Goes to Sea*

*Jenny's Birthday Book*

*Jenny's Moonlight Adventure*

*The School for Cats*


**JAMES CLOYD BOWMAN**

*Pecos Bill: The Greatest Cowboy of All Time*


**PALMER BROWN**

*Beyond the Pawpaw Trees*

*Cheerful*

*Hickory*

*The Silver Nutmeg*

*Something for Christmas*


**SHEILA BURNFORD**

*Bel Ria: Dog of War*


**DINO BUZZATI**

*The Bears' Famous Invasion of Sicily*


**CARLO COLLODI and FULVIO TESTA**

*Pinocchio*


**INGRI and EDGAR PARIN D'AULAIRE**

*D'Aulaires' Book of Animals*

*D'Aulaires' Book of Norse Myths*

*D'Aulaires' Book of Trolls*

*Foxie: The Singing Dog*

*The Terrible Troll-Bird*

*Too Big*

*The Two Cars*


**EILÍS DILLON**

*The Island of Horses*

*The Lost Island*


**ELEANOR FARJEON**

*The Little Bookroom*

PENELOPE FARMER
*Charlotte Sometimes*

PAUL GALLICO
*The Abandoned*

RUMER GODDEN
*An Episode of Sparrows*
*The Mousewife*

LUCRETIA P. HALE
*The Peterkin Papers*

RUSSELL and LILLIAN HOBAN
*The Sorely Trying Day*

RUTH KRAUSS and MARC SIMONT
*The Backward Day*

MUNRO LEAF and ROBERT LAWSON
*Wee Gillis*

RHODA LEVINE and EDWARD GOREY
*He Was There from the Day We Moved In*
*Three Ladies Beside the Sea*

BETTY JEAN LIFTON and EIKOH HOSOE
*Taka-chan and I*

NORMAN LINDSAY
*The Magic Pudding*

ERIC LINKLATER
*The Wind on the Moon*

J. P. MARTIN
*Uncle*
*Uncle Cleans Up*

JOHN MASEFIELD
*The Box of Delights*
*The Midnight Folk*

WILLIAM McCLEERY and WARREN CHAPPELL
*Wolf Story*

E. NESBIT
*The House of Arden*

DANIEL PINKWATER
*Lizard Music*

ALASTAIR REID and BOB GILL
*Supposing…*

ALASTAIR REID and BEN SHAHN
*Ounce Dice Trice*

BARBARA SLEIGH
*Carbonel and Calidor*
*Carbonel: The King of the Cats*
*The Kingdom of Carbonel*

E. C. SPYKMAN
*Terrible, Horrible Edie*

FRANK TASHLIN
*The Bear That Wasn't*

JAMES THURBER
*The 13 Clocks*
*The Wonderful O*

ALISON UTTLEY
*A Traveller in Time*

T. H. WHITE
*Mistress Masham's Repose*

MARJORIE WINSLOW and ERIK BLEGVAD
*Mud Pies and Other Recipes*

REINER ZIMNIK
*The Bear and the People*